# It Was Kit

The 'True Story of Christopher Marlowe

By: **Allison McWood**

Annelid Press

It Was Kit: The 'True' Story of Christopher Marlowe
Copyright © 2020 by Allison McWood.
FIRST EDITION

Cover photo by: Melissa-Jane Shaw

Edited by: Johnny Vong, Daniel Staheli

Featuring Original Cast Members: Kevin Risk, Kelsey Matheson, Chris Coculuzzi, Melissa-Jane Shaw, John Healy, Chantal Groulx

ISBN: 978-1-7771360-1-7

# Cast List

KIT MARLOWE......................................A playwright

THOMAS KYD .......................................His roommate

WILL SHAKESPEARE .............................A playwright

ROBERT GREENE ..................................A playwright

INGRAM FRIZER ...................................A spy

NICHOLAS SKERES...............................A spy

BLOB POLEY..........................................A spy

DICK BAINES ........................................A counterfeiter

JOHN MARLOWE...................................Kit's father

CATHERINE ARTHUR ............................Kit's mother

ANNE HATHAWAY ...............................Will's wife

ELEANOR BULL......................................Owner of a rooming house

QUEEN ELIZABETH ...............................The Queen

DANBY ..................................................A coroner

OFFICER 1/ATHEIST 1/TAMBURLAINE

OFFICER 2/ATHEIST 2/FAUSTUS

## Act One, Scene One

THOMAS          Kit! *(enters)* There is a dead rat in my doublet. Why did you do it?

KIT             You're always blaming everything on me.

THOMAS          You're the only roommate I have, Kit. There's no one else to blame.

KIT             You know what your problem is, Thomas? You have no sense of humour.

THOMAS          I fail to see the humour in finding dead vermin in my clothing.

KIT             I wanted to see what your reaction would be.

THOMAS          This is so like you. I don't understand why you find entertainment in making me furious with... What are you doing?

KIT             Cleaning up.

THOMAS          Who are you and what have you done with Kit?

KIT          My parents are coming to visit.

THOMAS       Good Ud, no.

KIT          Would you shut your yap and give me a hand?

*Knock at the door.*

KIT          That couldn't be them already. *(answers door)* Will.

WILL         I brought the script!

KIT          Will, this is not a good time.

WILL         If I have to wait any longer to work on a play with you, I might soil myself.

THOMAS       Pleasant. Now if you gentlemen will excuse me, I'm going to dispose of this rat. *(exits)*

WILL         I was up all night working on this draft. Tell me what you think.

KIT          Listen, Will. I don't have much time left.

WILL         Just skim it.  I'll be forever in your debt.

KIT          Will!

WILL          I look up to you! You are so brave! So innovative. So...so well dressed!

KIT             Will...

WILL            You are three months my elder, but eons ahead of me in insight.

KIT             Will...

WILL            I want to BE you!

KIT             No you don't.

WILL            I want to think like you, dress like you, but most of all I want to write plays the way you do. Please help me with my play.

KIT             I don't have ti...

WILL            *(getting on his knees)* I am your spaniel!

KIT             Will, please, no. Not the spaniel thing again.

WILL            (sitting up like a dog) Bark.

KIT             Will, this is not necess...

WILL            Bark.

KIT             Your embarrassing yoursel...

WILL            Bark.

KIT             For the love of Ud, Will! Don't make me hurt you!

WILL        Whimper.

KIT         *(sigh)* What's the working title.

WILL        Oh! I knew I could count on you, Kit! Because that's the
            kind of guy you are!

KIT         Don't hug me. What's the working title?

WILL         Romeo and Juliet.

KIT         ...Right.

WILL        Go ahead. Skim...Skim, skim, skim.

                              *As KIT skims through the script, he
                              tries to suppress laughter. WILL
                              absorbs KIT's every expression.
                              KIT lets out a stifled chortle.*

WILL        What? What's funny? What?

KIT         It's...cute.

WILL        Cute? I wasn't going for cute. But cute's good. Now is
            that your honest opinion?

KIT         Not entirely.

WILL        Be merciful, Kit! I'm dying here! Tell me what you really
            think! I can take it! What!

KIT         This is the corniest play I have ever read in my life.

WILL          What?

KIT           Will, this play stinks of cheese.

WILL          What's wrong with it?

KIT           It's fluff. It's mushy. It's a girl's play. What are you? A girl?

WILL          I don't know what to say.

KIT           I would never write a play like this.

WILL          It's a love story.

KIT           I don't write about love. I write about hatred.

WILL          And that's what's so endearing about you. Maybe if we collaborated...

KIT           I can't. You know how vain I am. To collaborate would mean I would have to share the credit and that is totally out of character for me. Besides, this is your play.

WILL          OUR play.

KIT           No, Will. It's yours. I can't put my name on this. It's not my style. Sure, there's slaughter and suicide. And I approve of that. But there's not enough destruction. It's not over-the-top. It's not dangerous.

WILL          I can be dangerous! I can be dangerous like you! We have a lot more in common than you think.

KIT          Will, pay attention. We are not...the same...person.

WILL         Oh, fie.

*ROBERT invites himself in.*

ROBERT       Greetings, Christopher! How is the best dressed playwright in England?

KIT          I'm well, Robert...Wait a minute. Didn't you die last year?

ROBERT       I dropped by to see if my favourite colleague would like to join me at the tavern where we can have drinks and discuss how obscenely intelligent we are.

WILL         May I come too, Mr. Greene?

ROBERT       What is he doing here? Who let him in?

KIT          Both of you, please! I'm running out of time!

ROBERT       *(to WILL)* Thou tripe! Thou disease! Thou uneducated eel!

WILL         Please stop calling me 'thou.' It makes me uncomfortable.

ROBERT       Christopher, what did I tell you about fraternizing with swine? Ignorance is contagious, you know.

WILL          I agree with you, Mr. Greene.

KIT            He's filling theatres.

WILL          Can't argue with you there.

ROBERT     I wouldn't stand in the penny yard to watch his drivel.

WILL          I don't blame you.

KIT            I agree his plays are fluffy, but the rest of England seems to like them.

WILL          Absolutely.

ROBERT     He's not like us, Christopher. He didn't go to Cambridge. He's not part of the educated elite. Who does he think he is, hogging our audiences? Pure travesty!

WILL          He has a point, Kit.

KIT            Will, you can't keep agreeing with both of us.

WILL          I couldn't agree with you more.

KIT            Will...

WILL          I don't want to offend anyone.

ROBERT     *(to WILL)* Heed my warning. Keep your hindquarters out of the theatre! You don't belong here! Just because everyone loves your plays, doesn't mean they are any good.

KIT    You know something, Robert? You really should unwedge whatever it is you have stuck up your arse. And do it before my parents arrive.

WILL    Your parents are coming! How lovely! Can I stay and visit?

KIT    Absolutely not. Both of you, out!

*Knock at the door.*

KIT    You see? My parents are here already and not only am I ill prepared, I've got you two fops lingering around like a foul odour...Mom? Dad? Is that you?

DICK    *(from outside)* It's me!

KIT    It's Richard Baines! Hide!

*Everyone hides.*

DICK    I know you're in there! Open up, will you?

*KIT reluctantly opens the door.*

KIT    Dick.

DICK    I go by Richard, actually. People don't call me Dick.

KIT    That's what you think.

DICK              Robert. Will. Make yourselves scarce. I have something
                  of great importance to discuss with Kit.

WILL              We were just leaving.

ROBERT            If there's one thing you can do, Dick, it's clear a room.

                  *Exit WILL and ROBERT*

DICK              Mind if I help myself to some ale? Don't mind if I do.

                  *Helps himself to ale.*

KIT               Don't drink that! I'll have nothing to offer my parents!

DICK              Didn't your parents teach you to share?

KIT               What was I thinking? I'm sure my parents won't mind
                  drinking from the chamber pot.

DICK              Let's get down to business. Kit, I like you. Hang me, I
                  LIKE you. That's why I'm letting you in on a little
                  business negotiation. Kit, how would you like to...

KIT               No.

DICK              I can make you a wealthy man. Think of it, Kit. You
                  could move out of this seedy neighbourhood. And
                  think of all the pretty clothes you could buy.

KIT               I like living in the Liberties, and my brother-in-law is a
                  tailor.

DICK   Let me explain something to you...

KIT   You've been counterfeiting again, haven't you?

DICK   Don't call it counterfeiting. It makes me sound dishonest.

KIT   I'll none of it, Dick. You've gotten me in trouble with the law in the past for illicit coining. You will not cozen me into it again.

DICK   This ale is horrible. *(dumps ale on the floor)*

KIT   Dick! I have an urge to crack this bottle over your skull!

DICK   Take a number. So, can I call you a partner?

KIT   You are not to be trusted.

DICK   You're overreacting.

KIT   You tried to wipe out an entire seminary by poisoning their drinking water.

DICK   Come on, Kit! The Queen is after me again. I need someone to help me save face, and you are the smartest man I know!

KIT   Out!

*KIT pushes DICK out the door. KIT leaves the room.*

DICK          *(from outside)* Kit! I'll make it worth your while! Kit!...Kit?

> *When KIT does not answer, DICK opens the door and peaks around the corner. Once he sees that no one is around, he sneaks into the apartment and hides in a cupboard.*

## Act One, Scene Two

> INGRAM, NICHOLAS AND BLOB
> are hiding in the bushes outside
> KIT's apartment.

INGRAM          What's he doing now?

BLOB            (looking through the window) He's wiping a puddle of
                ale from the floor.

NICHOLAS        How can an ex-spy lead such a boring life?

BLOB            Hey. This is Christopher Marlowe we're talking about.
                Give him some time. He'll eventually do something
                offensive.

NICHOLAS        Who would have guessed we would ever get to spy on
                a former colleague?

BLOB            I'm confused. Why does the Queen want us to spy on
                Kit?

INGRAM          The Queen heard a rumour that Marlowe is a double
                agent. She's afraid for her life.

NICHOLAS        How a propos. The three of us spying on a suspected
                double agent. We, being double agents ourselves.

Blob, do you remember the year of 1586?

NICHOLAS & BLOB   *(dreamily)* The Babington Plot.

INGRAM          I missed that one.

BLOB            How could you possibly miss the Babington Plot?

NICHOLAS        Don't you have any experience in intelligence work?

INGRAM          I have no record of intelligence.

NICHOLAS        But it was the BABINGTON Plot!

BLOB            Oh, Ingram, it was thrilling! You should have been there!

NICHOLAS        Espionage at its finest!

BLOB            We plotted against the Queen's life in an attempt to...

NICHOLAS        ...replace her with Mary Queen of ...

BLOB            ...Scots! And all of the conspirators were executed.

NICHOLAS        Except us, of course.

BLOB            Because we're sneaky.

INGRAM          I envy you, gentlemen. Nothing is more amusing than split loyalties.

NICHOLAS          Don't feel bad, Ingram. You're not a bad little liar yourself.

INGRAM            Oh, Nicholas. You're just saying that.

NICHOLAS          Come on, Mr. Conny-Catching Loan Shark. What about all those unassuming, rich gentlemen you cheated. You should see this guy in action, Blob. He's brilliant. He charges wealthy gentlemen one hundred percent interest on their loans. If they can't pay the interest, he forfeits their property. And here's the kicker. The loans are never forthcoming.

BLOB              You jest.

NICHOLAS          If I speak the truth, may I never tell a lie again. I'm a big fan of Ingram's work. It's a hobby of mine to act as his frequent accomplice. You would be proud, Blob. I am the one who identifies and lures those foolish gentlemen into Ingram's trap.

INGRAM            I couldn't do it without you, Nicholas.

BLOB              I'll admit, it takes savvy to be a moneylender, but it takes pure genius to be a pathological liar.

NICHOLAS          He's got you there, Ingram. Blob has mastered the art of lying. He is a most cunning counterfeiter and dissembler. A notable knave with no trust in him.

BLOB              Oh! You flatter me!

INGRAM            Are you telling me you're pathological?

BLOB            Would I lie about something like that?

INGRAM          Prove it.

BLOB            Okay. I will...I am fond of the Queen.

NICHOLAS        Oh! That was a good one, Blob! You really had me going there for a minute.

BLOB            Notice how I looked you straight in the face when I said that? Not a flinch.

INGRAM          Not bad. I wasn't entirely convinced, but...

BLOB            What do you mean you were not entirely convinced? I can lie convincingly under any circumstances. I can look the Queen herself right in the eyes and lie to her ugly face. And I have! On more than one occasion. What about the Babington Plot?

INGRAM          Would you let it go? That stupid Babington Plot was over a long time ago!

BLOB            What's his problem?

NICHOLAS        Don't brag too much about being a better liar than Ingram. He's a bit sensitive about that.

BLOB            Fie on me. Listen, Ingram, I'm sorry. You are every bit as good a liar as I am.

NICHOLAS        Damn, he's good! Blob Poley, you are the master!

INGRAM          Oh! For the love of Ud!

## Act One, Scene Three

*KIT is wiping ale from the floor in his apartment. Enter THOMAS.*

KIT         It's about time. I could have used your help, you know.

THOMAS      They're your parents.

KIT         What took you so long, anyway? How long could it take to dispose of a dead rat?

THOMAS      I didn't exactly dispose of him.

KIT         Him? Since when did this dead rat go from being an it to a him?

THOMAS      Stuff happens.

KIT         So if you didn't dispose of the rat, what did you do?

THOMAS      I took him to the tavern.

KIT         What for?

THOMAS      Drinks.

KIT     You took a dead rat to the tavern?

THOMAS    Could you please not call him the dead rat anymore? His name is Stiffy.

KIT     You named him?

THOMAS    I was going to get rid of him. I was! I went to the riverbank, took Stiffy by the tail and was just about to fling him, when something came over me. I looked into his little face. And...well...I sort of felt sorry for him. I realized that I could relate to this rat. I am a lot like this rat. This rat and I have a lot in common.

KIT     In what sense?

THOMAS    I've invited Stiffy to live here with us, Kit. I told him you wouldn't mind.

KIT     You are not keeping a dead rat in our apartment.

THOMAS    His name is Stiffy.

KIT     Thomas, that rat is going to decompose and start to stink.

THOMAS    Someday you'll decompose and start to stink.

KIT     Yes, but when that happens, I don't plan on living here.

THOMAS    Kit, this is something I have to do. Whenever I look at this rat, I get this weird feeling. I feel overcome with guilt.

KIT            Guilt?

THOMAS         I wasn't there for Stiffy when he was alive. I want to spend the rest of my life making it up to him.

KIT            That's noble, Thomas. But my parents will be arriving soon, and if there is a dead rat in the apartment, it will be yet another thing for us to fight about.

THOMAS         He'll behave.

*Knock at the door.*

KIT            That must be my parents. Hide that thing, will you?

*KIT answers the door to reveal two men.*

ATHEIST 1      Good afternoon. We represent the London chapter of the Atheist Brigade. Our mission is to go door to door, spreading atheism to misinformed Christians. Are you a misinformed Christian?

KIT            I'm afraid you're wasting your time.

ATHEIST 2      That's where you're wrong. We are the bearers of good news. Wouldn't you like to live with the peace of mind that when you die, absolutely nothing will happen?

ATHEIST 1      And won't it be easier to sleep at night knowing that the earth is being randomly hurled around in space with no higher power to keep it secure?

KIT            I'm not listening. I...

ATHEIST 2      Atheism promises an eternity of nothingness, along with a satisfying void that most people so mindlessly fill with spirituality.

ATHEIST 1      Would you like to share in our joy as we experience this void together?

KIT            You understand that what you are doing is a felony.

ATHEIST 2      We are doing it for the greater good.

ATHEIST 1      It will only take a moment of your time. All you have to do is join hands with us now and say the Sinner's Prayer backwards.

KIT            You can't tell me what to believe!

ATHEIST 2      This poor man has a soul. It makes me all weepy.

ATHEIST 1      Why don't we just leave you these brochures. Perhaps if you read them, you will come to your senses and change your mind. Good day.

ATHEIST 2      *(on their way out)* And you can be assured that neither one of us will be praying for you.

                          *Exit Atheists.*

THOMAS         What was that all about?

KIT            It was the Atheist Brigade. They left us more of this bloody, Atheist literature.

THOMAS          Again?

KIT             Just put it in the closet with the rest of them.

*Knock at the door.*

KIT             Those Atheists never give up! *(answers door)* How many times do I have to tell you, I am not an Atheist!

JOHN            That's good to know.

KIT             Mom. Dad.

*Exit THOMAS.*

JOHN            Good to see you, Son. *(hands KIT shoes)* Here. Have some shoes.

CATHERINE       My adorable, baby boy!

JOHN            So, Kit. When are you going to get a real job?

KIT             Congratulations, Dad. It only took you twelve seconds this time.

CATHERINE       Have you met a nice girl yet, Kitty?

KIT             Mom...

JOHN            Shoes. That's where the money is, son. Everyone needs shoes. You are a Marlowe, and Marlowe men make shoes.

KIT          I've been doing well for myself. The Admiral's Men have been performing some of my work. In fact, they're doing *Dr. Faustus* right now. I was going to invite you to...

JOHN       *Dr. Faustus?* Is that the play with the Jew, the racist, the devil or the queer?

KIT          YOU read my work?

JOHN       Your mother says I should be supportive. So which is it?

KIT          The one with the devil.

JOHN       My son. The devil-lover.

KIT          I do not love the devil.

JOHN       No. You just write plays about him.

KIT          There are nuns in *The Jew of Malta*. Does that make me a nun?

JOHN       Apparently not if you go around writing plays about the devil.

CATHERINE   You can meet lots of nice people selling shoes, Kitty. Lady people.

KIT          I don't want to be a shoemaker!

JOHN            Would you listen to that, Catherine? My first born son
                would rather prance around on a stage in his leotards
                than take me up on the invaluable shoe empire I built
                for him. What's wrong, Kit?  You too good to be a
                Marlowe?

CATHERINE       There is no shame in shoe business. Your father is a
                member of the Shoemaker and Tanner's Guild.

KIT             What in frigging hell am I going to do with a profuse
                education in Classical Literature if I'm making shoes?

JOHN            Don't think education makes you better than a
                shoemaker, because it doesn't, you pompous, little
                brat!

KIT             You think I'M pompous? Ever since you became a clerk
                at St. Mary's, you strut around like you're some sort of
                evangelist!

DICK            (peaking from the cupboard, writing something down)
                John the Evangelist.

CATHERINE       (lets out a scream) The agony! The agony! To see my
                two best boys fighting like mongrels in the street! Woe
                is me! Woe! Woe!

JOHN            Stop being so dramatic, Catherine.

CATHERINE       You two used to be as close-knit as netherstocks. John,
                do you remember when Kitty was wee? He was so
                afraid of thunder, he used to crawl into bed with you
                on stormy nights. Remember how cute he was?

DICK            *(writing)* ...Bedfellow to John the Evangelist.

KIT             Nobody, not even my own father can tell me how to
                live my life. I am a free thinker!

JOHN            You're not old enough to be a free thinker. You're only
                twelve years old!

KIT             I'm twenty-nine!

JOHN            As far as your mother and I are concerned, you're
                twelve!

CATHERINE       Kitty, why is there a hole in your wall?

THOMAS          *(entering)* It was Kit.

KIT             Thomas, go away.

THOMAS          Kit got mad and put his fist through the wall.

KIT             There you go, blaming me again.

THOMAS          Kit has a vicious temper.

JOHN            Must get it from his mother's side.

CATHERINE       I'm worried, Kitty.

KIT             Oh, here we go.

CATHERINE       We have discussed your tantrums before.

KIT          Mom...

CATHERINE    And another thing. I don't think I approve of this neighborhood you live in.

KIT          What's wrong with the Liberties?

CATHERINE    On our way here we saw two very friendly young ladies who were almost completely naked.

JOHN        Arrroooo!

CATHERINE    I'm worried.

KIT          There's nothing to worry about.

CATHERINE    I'm concerned they might be cold. Maybe you should loan them some of your clothes, Kitty. You always have such nice clothes.

JOHN        And where, might I ask did you get the money to purchase such lavish attire? Answer me, Mr. Fancy-Pants. Where does a playwright find that kind of money?

THOMAS      He and Dick Baines were involved in a counterfeiting scheme a couple of years back.

KIT          You little snitch!

CATHERINE    Dick Baines. I don't approve of him, Kitty. He's a bad influence.

DICK            *(inside cupboard, speaking in stage whisper)* That's not true! You dishonest wench!

JOHN            My son is a counterfeiting bastard!

DICK            *(writing)* ...Bastard. His mother dishonest.

JOHN            What other trouble has my son been getting into, Thomas?

THOMAS          Not much. Unless you count the time he was arrested for murder.

JOHN            What!

CATHERINE       *(face down, pounding her fists on the floor)* Lordy! Lordy! Lordy! I've given birth to a murderer!

KIT             I wasn't charged!

THOMAS          He started a tavern brawl.

KIT             Why is it that every time I happen to be present at a tavern brawl, everyone thinks I'm the one who started it?

THOMAS          I don't know, Kit. Could it be your lewd mouth and violent temper?

KIT             I never hurt anyone.

THOMAS          He's always attempting sudden privy injury to men.

KIT               It's my sharp tongue that causes injury.

JOHN              So, about this brawl...

KIT               I was trying to break it up! Watson the poet got in a tiff with Bradley the inn-keeper's son. I tried to...

JOHN              So it was a poet. It's always a poet.

CATHERINE         Why can't you be more like Will Shakespeare? He's such a nice boy.

KIT               Mother...

CATHERINE         He's married, Kitty. And has three children.

KIT               Come on, Mom! Two of them are twins. They only count as one.

CATHERINE         Level with me, Kitty. Will I ever be a grandmother?

KIT               Stop pressuring me!

CATHERINE         Is something not functioning? Do you need to see a doctor?

KIT               That's enough!

CATHERINE         Why, Kitty? All I want to know is why? Why are you denying me my fundamental right to watch my son crank out miniature versions of himself?

KIT                It's my business!

CATHERINE          Why?

KIT                Because I...

CATHERINE          Why?

KIT                It's not what I...

CATHERINE          Why...

KIT                Because I...Because...Because I prefer men. That's it. I prefer men.

THOMAS             Holy crap!

DICK               *(writing vigorously)* This is too easy.

KIT                Mother? Mother, speak to me.

CATHERINE          I've failed! I've failed! I've failed!

JOHN               *(stuffing a shoe in her mouth)* Stuff it, Catherine.

KIT                That's right. This is why I'm not married. And anyone who loves not tobacco and boys are fools.

DICK               *(writing)* You are so quotable, Kit.

JOHN               *(taking KIT aside)* Son, can I have a word with you a moment? *(cuffs him on the head)* Have you fallen on your head?

KIT       What!

JOHN      You're queer, just like that king in your play!

> CATHERINE swoons and falls into THOMAS' arms. THOMAS tends to her.

JOHN      You know what  they do with queers? They use them for kindling, that's what they do!

KIT       Dad, I am not gay!

JOHN      But you just said that...

KIT       I said that so Mom would stop harassing me to get married.

JOHN      You lied to your mother.

KIT       It wasn't a lie...exactly...It was more...irony.

JOHN      Don't use those fancy Cambridge words with me, boy. I know a lie when I hear one.

KIT       It's not a fancy Cambridge word. It's irony. I was being ironic. I was saying the opposite of what I mean to make a point.

JOHN      Sounds like a lie to me.

KIT              It's a playwriting technique.

JOHN             Well, here's a shoemaker's technique. Say what you mean! This irony as you call it, is going to land you in serious trouble! You  mark my  words! Now where are you taking us for dinner?

KIT              *(sigh)* Get your cloaks.

                                    *Exit KIT and JOHN. THOMAS drags CATHERINE out. Once everyone is gone, DICK comes out of the cupboard and speaks to the audience.*

DICK             I've got it all here, in my own handwriting. This will create quite a diversion. The Queen won't waste her time interrogating a meager counterfeiter when there is a blaspheming heathen right under her nose. Marlowe will be sorry he didn't help me out with my ploy. How sweet it is to savour revenge while simultaneously keeping my arse from being hanged. Might as well break two heads with one mace.

THOMAS           *(re-entering)* Are you talking to yourself again, Dick?

DICK             Thomas! No one was here, so I let myself in. I peed in the corner. I hope you don't mind.

THOMAS           Why have you plagued us with your presence?

DICK             I was looking for something.

THOMAS           Did you find it?

DICK                Oh, yes. I did.

# ACT ONE, SCENE FOUR

*A tavern. WILL is seated at a table with KIT. WILL has a quill and paper. KIT has his head buried in his arms.*

KIT     Wench! More ale!

WILL    So about Romeo and Juliet.

KIT     Another time, Will.

WILL    But I...

         *Enter ROBERT.*

ROBERT   What ho! Christopher! How pleasant to...*(sees WILL)* What is the meaning of this?

KIT     Moan.

ROBERT   This is OUR table, Christopher! This is where the two of us sit and discuss lofty matters. What could a famous gracer of tragedians be doing here with this maggot?

KIT     My head is swimming. *(flops head back in his arms)*

ROBERT    *(to WILL)* Thou virus. Thou flea. Thou illiterate bard.

WILL    Would you like to read my play, Mr. Greene?

ROBERT    I've read your work, Shakespeare. And I've seen more tantalizing morsels in my own vomit.

WILL    I'm sure you had a good reason for saying that.

ROBERT    I warned you to stop infecting our theatres with this brain-numbing puke you so you so ignorantly refer to as drama.

WILL    I value your opinion, Mr. Greene. But nonetheless, people seem to be swarming like flies to see my plays.

ROBERT    Flies don't swarm to theatres. They swarm around in circles until they find manure to land on.

WILL    That is a clever analogy.

ROBERT    I deserve success, not you! I will give you one last chance. Go back to Stratford where you belong!

WILL    But...

ROBERT    You are no genius. *(pulls KIT's head up by the hair, revealing KIT making a stupid, drunk face)* Now THIS is the face of a genius.

WILL    I never said I was a genius. I'm just an ordinary guy who likes writing plays.

ROBERT      They are not plays. They are shallow puddles.  Away with you, thou ruffian. Thou mongrel. Thou menstrual rag!

WILL        That reminds me. I need to send a missive to my wife. My twins are having a birthday.

*Exit WILL. ROBERT sits next to KIT.*

ROBERT      Christopher?

KIT         Grunt.

ROBERT      Shakespeare must be destroyed.

KIT         Sure thing, Robert.

ROBERT      I did not pursue a higher education only to skulk in the shadow of that buffoon.

KIT         Belch.

ROBERT      I heard that Shakespeare has taken an interest in writing sonnets. Well, so have I.

KIT         Sssonnets.

ROBERT      I have written a collection of 154 sonnets, and have signed Shakespeare's name on them.

KIT         Lots of pretty sonnets.

ROBERT      Oh, these are better than anything Shakespeare could ever write. Especially the ones a about the mistress.

KIT           Are you sure you're not dead?

ROBERT        I'm sure there's a little lady in Stratford who would like
              to read these sonnets. Surely she would like to know
              what her loyal husband is up to.

KIT           Need ale.

ROBERT        I'm sending my masterpiece to Stratford. Today.
              Shakespeare will wish he had heeded my warning.

# ACT ONE, SCENE FIVE

> *INGRAM, NICHOLAS and BLOB are in the bushes.*

INGRAM        Someone's coming!

> *DICK enters. There is a disappointed moan among the spies.*

DICK        What are you guys doing in the bushes?

BLOB        We could tell you, but then we'd have to kill you.

NICHOLAS        That's not a bad idea, actually.

BLOB        Good point. We have been sent to spy on Christopher Marlowe.

DICK        Spies? Do you work for the Queen?

NICHOLAS        At times.

INGRAM        Let's kill him now.

DICK        Before you kill me, I have something that could be of some value to you.

BLOB            What say you?

DICK            I have evidence that Christopher Marlowe is a heretic.
                A homosexual one at that.

INGRAM          Solid evidence?

DICK            Define solid.

NICHOLAS        This is not a game, little man. The Queen isn't going to
                be interested in flimsy evidence.

DICK            I was hiding in Marlowe's cupboard and I wrote down
                everything he said.

INGRAM          *(taking notes from DICK)* Let me see this...I don't
                understand your shorthand. You keep writing a capital
                letter 'C.' What does the capital letter 'C' signify?

DICK            You are spies. You figure it out.

                              Exit DICK. The spies examine the
                              notes.

INGRAM          The capital letter 'C.'

NICHOLAS        You morons. It must stand for Christopher.

BLOB            Or Christ.

INGRAM          Blob has a point. 'Christopher' makes no sense in the
                context. 'Christ' sounds better. Listen to this..."A note
                regarding the opinion of one Christopher Marlowe

concerning his damnable judgement of religion and scorn of God's word." He says "that St. John the Evangelist was bedfellow to 'C.' That 'C' was a bastard and his mother dishonest."

BLOB    Didn't I tell you? That filthy heathen is talking about Christ!

INGRAM    And down here it says "all they that love not tobacco and boys are fools."

NICHOLAS    Did Marlowe really say that?

BLOB    What difference does it make? We have it written down.

NICHOLAS    It's payday, Gentelmen! Let's take this to the Queen.

INGRAM    Not so fast. What we hold in our hands is blasphemy. An overt attack on God. If the Queen finds this in our possession...

NICHOLAS    She'll think it's an attack on her. Because she thinks she is God.

INGRAM    She might assume that we had something to do with this.

BLOB    We'll be accused of treason.

NICHOLAS    And hanged.

INGRAM    And that won't look too good on our record.

BLOB          So what do we do?

INGRAM        These notes need to be found in Marlowe's possession. We'll plant them in his apartment.

NICHOLAS      We'll go to the Queen and tell her we have reason to believe that Marlowe is plotting treason.

BLOB          We'll request that she issue a search warrant.

INGRAM        They'll find the notes.

NICHOLAS      And the Queen will give us a beefy raise.

BLOB          This is such fun!

## Act One, Scene Six

*The apartment. KIT is lying limply in a chair.*

THOMAS  Stiffy wants to know why you never told us that you prefer men. He feels that if he is going to live here with us, he has a right to be informed of any major liabilities.

KIT  That rat has a lot to say.

THOMAS  You're not being fair to Stiffy.

KIT  If Stiffy wasn't already dead, I'd...

THOMAS  You are so temperamental.

KIT  I wouldn't be temperamental if I wasn't surrounded by so many irritating people.

THOMAS  I can understand why you didn't tell Stiffy. You hardly know him. But why didn't you tell me? Did you think I would think less of you? Did you think I would turn you in?

KIT  I am not gay.

THOMAS          You're not gay? OH. This is so like you.

KIT             Brace yourself. I feel a sarcastic insult coming on.

THOMAS          This is one of your pranks, isn't it? You're going around saying you're gay just to see how many people you can get a rise out of.

KIT             Not exactly. But those would be happy results.

THOMAS          Don't deny it. I know you. Everything you do has to be like a wet fish in the face. Over the top. Larger than life. Shocking! This sort of thing may work in your plays, but its annoying as hell when you have to live with it day after day!

KIT             I'm about due for a public disturbance. May I leave now, or would that be rude?

THOMAS          You have got to stop living as though you are a character in one of your plays.

KIT             I don't do that.

THOMAS          Good Ud! Sometimes I think you have completely confused reality with drama. Isn't that right, Stiffy?

                                    *KIT throws STIFFY out the window.*

KIT             You want to be next?

THOMAS          I can't believe you just did that.

KIT                 The rat had it coming.

THOMAS              You're trying to make me mad.

KIT                 It's so easy to do.

THOMAS              I'm having a nervous breakdown!

KIT                 I'm having a hangover. Want to trade?

THOMAS              You are impossible!

KIT                 You haven't shut up yet.

THOMAS              I am going to retrieve Stiffy.

KIT                 Don't bother coming back.

                                    *Exit THOMAS.*

KIT                 Ah! Solitude!

                                    *TAMBURLAINE appears.*

TAMBURLAINE  He's right, you know.

KIT                 Not you again.

TAMBURLAINE  I'm in your imagination. You can't escape me.

KIT                 Even in my imagination I can't find peace.

TAMBURLAINE   Peace? You? The king of civil unrest?

KIT           Listen, Tamburlaine, I wrote you and I can erase you.

TAMBURLAINE   You can't. I'm part of who you are.

KIT           I am nothing like you.

TAMBURLAINE   Thomas was right. You are synonymous with the characters in your plays.

KIT           I am not a sadistic killer like yourself! I never killed anyone!

TAMBURLAINE   You didn't have to. I did it for you.

KIT           Tamburlaine...

TAMBURLAINE   We are the same. Face it. We're both overreachers. Grabbing what we want.

KIT           I worked hard for everything I have!

TAMBURLAINE   You were a shoemaker's son. I was a shepherd. You think no one will make the connection?

KIT           You don't understand. I...

TAMBURLAINE   You want to be the Father of Drama. To brand your insignia on the theatre's flank. To change the very essence of dramatic literature as we know it.

KIT            So what's wrong with...

TAMBURLAINE    I want to rule the world.

KIT            You're just as bad as everyone else, you know that?
               You think you have me figured out because of the plays
               I write. That's not fair.

TAMBURLAINE    You mean to tell me that parts of yourself never end up
               in your characters? You are lying to yourself.

KIT            You don't know me. You don't know anything about
               me! Nobody does!

TAMBURLAINE    I know you as well as I know myself. We are the same,
               only I'm better.

KIT            What the...

TAMBURLAINE    You made me a hero.

KIT            I made you a burlesque. I was making fun of...

TAMBURLAINE    People think I'm a hero.

KIT            Only because they don't understand what I was trying
               to do. I was trying something different. Nobody has
               ever done this sort of thing before.

TAMBURLAINE    Irony is dangerous, Marlowe. Of late, people have
               posted racist threats on church doors, and have done it
               in the name of Tamburlaine.

KIT              I have no control over how people react to my work.

TAMBURLAINE   Your efforts have backfired.

KIT              Out, scab! Get out of my mind!

TAMBURLAINE   It's too late. I am in control now. I have taken possession of your thoughts. You will never escape. Stoop thou, and be footstool to great Tamburlaine!

KIT              NO!

                          *FAUSTUS appears.*

FAUSTUS          Why don't you just leave him alone?

TAMBURLAINE   Faustus?

FAUSTUS          Like the poor guy hasn't been through enough as it is. Marlowe, I know exactly how you feel.

KIT              I will not stand here and be defended by a fictitious character.

FAUSTUS          Would you look at that? He's in denial. I was in denial once.

KIT              Denial?

FAUSTUS          Denial about selling your soul to the devil.

KIT              I did no such thing.

FAUSTUS    Poor wretch. Do you want a hug? Here. Let me give you a hug.

KIT    Why are you hugging me?

FAUSTUS    I am comforting you in the last meager moments you have on this earth. You are going straight to hell.

KIT    What say you?

FAUSTUS    You sold your soul to the devil.

KIT    That wasn't me. That was you.

FAUSTUS    When you were at Cambridge you renounced everything that was important to you for the sake of acquiring knowledge. You gave up your family.

KIT    I wanted more than the life of a simple shoemaker.

FAUSTUS    You prostituted your morals.

KIT    What morals?

FAUSTUS    You worked as a spy to put yourself through school.

KIT    Students always get the shit jobs.

FAUSTUS    You gave up on God.

KIT    The church disappointed me. Not God.

FAUSTUS        Was it worth it? Was it worth selling your soul for knowledge?

KIT            Why must you insist...

TAMBURLAINE    Maybe YOU are a character in a play. Ever think of that, Marlowe? Who's to say you are not the product of someone's imagination.

FAUSTUS        Don't freak him out.

TAMBURLAINE    Marlowe, your life is no different than any of the twisted plots you thought up. Do you think someone wrote YOU?

FAUSTUS        Listen, you verbose bag of self-importance, there is no point in worsening his lot. His time is almost up.

KIT            What do you mean by that?

                              *TAMBURLAINE and FAUSTUS disappear.*

KIT            What do you mean my time is...Faustus? Tamburlaine!

# Act One, Scene Seven

*INGRAM is alone in the bushes.*

INGRAM      Every man must leave his mark. What about me? True, I am a lewd moneylender. A shark. I disrupt the lives of cocky, young gentlemen. But it's not the Babington Plot. Nicholas, Blob and that bloody Babington Plot. How can I compete with that? Then there's Marlowe with his controversial plays and public disturbances. That lucky bugger has trouble just falling in his lap. People will remember Marlowe and Nicholas and Blob. When I'm buried, my name will just vaporize and no one will ever remember I was alive. *(enter NICHOLAS)* What ho! Is the deed done?

NICHOLAS    It was too easy. I slipped into Marlowe's apartment and left the scandalous notes in his closet.

INGRAM      Good, good.

NICHOLAS    He was so engrossed in a conversation with William Shakespeare that neither one noticed I was there.

*BLOB rushes in.*

BLOB        The Queen has been informed!

NICHOLAS        Blob, you are a marvel!

BLOB            I looked the Queen straight in the face and told her about Marlowe's treacherous plottings. She turned a revolting shade of green!

NICHOLAS        Blob, I could hug you.

BLOB            Please don't.

INGRAM          I could have lied to the Queen too, you know. Hell, I could have planted the notes in Marlowe's closet. But instead, I was left alone in the bushes, twiddling my thumbs.

NICHOLAS        But you are so good at things like that.

BLOB            Excellent twiddling.

INGRAM          You don't think I'm a good spy.

NICHOLAS        Of course we do.

INGRAM          Enough of your pretense! I know what the two of you think of me. You think I'm a half ass spy with the balls of a neutered cat! I'll not be made to look like a court jester! I AM A SPY!

                                *ROBERT walks by and gives INGRAM a weird look.*

NICHOLAS        Nice going, Ingram.

BLOB            What part of  SECRET agent confuses you?

INGRAM          Fie.

# Act One, Scene Eight

*WILL and KIT are in KIT's apartment.*

WILL          How do fairies sound to you? Fairies frolicking in the forest, causing mischief among young lovers. Wouldn't fairies be fun, Kit?

KIT           Do your characters ever talk to you?

WILL          What say you?

KIT           The characters in your plays. Do they talk to you?

WILL          Titus Andronicus once appeared to me in a dream and slapped me. Then I remembered he didn't have a hand. But it made so much sense when I was dreaming it.

KIT           I'm not talking about dreams, Will. I mean, do your characters walk into your apartment and speak to you the way I'm speaking to you now?

WILL          Has this happened to you? OH! Your imagination puts me to shame!

KIT           Do you think about death?

WILL          I don't have much time to die, really. I busy myself
              mostly with living.

KIT           Surely you ponder death occasionally.

WILL          No. Living pretty much consumes most of my schedule.

                              *ROBERT enters, smirking.*

KIT           Robert? Why are you looking so smug?

ROBERT        No reason.

                              *ROBERT points to the door at the
                              exact moment someone knocks.*

WILL          Are you expecting someone, Kit?

ANNE          *(from outside)* Open up! I know you're in there, you
              double crossing bag of horse plop!

KIT           Will, is that your wife?

WILL          Anne? Is that you, my angelic one?

ANNE          Damn straight, it's me! Now open this door so I can
              break your head!

WILL          How wonderful! My little flower has journeyed all the
              way from Stratford to surprise me!

                              *WILL opens the door. As ANNE
                              storms in, ROBORT stands aside*

*and gloats.*

ANNE        I thought I might find you here, you little wank!

WILL        I'm sure you meant that affectionately.

ANNE        Where is she?

WILL        She who?

ANNE        That little whore you've been slamming!

WILL        I'm confused.

ANNE        How could you do this to me? How could you do this to little Judith and Hamnet?

WILL        Do what?

ANNE        You leave me alone in Stratford with a screaming brat on each hip, while you go gallivanting across London! You tell me you're away on business, when all the while you've been going hog wild in the brothels!

WILL        Never, my love! I am forever faithful!

ANNE        Save it! You have a mistress! Everyone knows about it now!

WILL        Scandal!

ANNE        They call her the Dark Lady. Since when did you prefer brunettes?

WILL You are the only one! You are my succulent pomegranate! My shapely gourd!

ANNE Eat worms! I read all about your little hussy in this book of sonnets you wrote!

WILL I wrote no sonnets.

ANNE I suppose you're going to tell me her eyes are like the sun!

WILL Her eyes are nothing like the sun!

ANNE SO I'VE READ!

WILL Let me come home with you to Stratford! I'll prove myself worthy...

ANNE Don't bother ever coming home! You are no longer welcome in my house! *(stops, noticing ROBERT)* Wait a minute. Didn't you die last year?...Never mind.

> *ANNE leaves, slamming the door behind her. WILL begins to whimper, and slam his head repeatedly against the wall.*

KIT Will, I don't know what to say.

WILL *(thrusting himself into KIT's arms)* Hold me.

KIT          Um, well...

ROBERT      Serves you right. Thou parasite. Thou fungus. Thou involuntary spasm.

KIT          Robert, were you behind this?

WILL        I have no mistress. What means this lady?

KIT          *(reading sonnets)* Robert, these sonnets are written in your hand.

ROBERT      I warned him. He brought this on himself! Yes! I wrote the sonnets! And Shakespeare deserved every couplet!

WILL        What did I ever do to you?

ROBERT      You mock me! With your success! With your humility! Everybody loves you and it makes me want to throw up!

WILL        Everybody loves me except the only person who matters.

ROBERT      OH, smeck up!

KIT          Get out of my house.

ROBERT      You don't mean that.

KIT          Out, scab! *(tossing ROBERT out)* And a thousand times, fie!

WILL          Aye me! I am out of her favour!

KIT          Listen, Will. Why don't you go back to your place and try to get your mind off things. You can write about your fairies. That will make you happy.

WILL          Please don't make me leave. I can't be alone right now.

KIT          What will you do, then?

WILL          Let me stay here with you. Oh, Kit, please! I can't be by myself!

KIT          There's not much room. I mean, since the dead rat moved in...

WILL          *(grabbing KIT's leg)* Only for one night!

KIT          Will, nature calls. Can I leave you alone for ten minutes while I go to the privy?

WILL          Don't leave me!

KIT          I can't very well take you along to the privy. Nine minutes then.

WILL          How can you defecate when my heart is breaking!

KIT          Let go of my leg before I mess my pants!

*Exit KIT.*

# Act One, Scene Nine

*INGRAM, NICHOLAS and BLOB are in the bushes. KIT walks by.*

INGRAM      Where do you think you're going?

KIT      I'm going to the privy.

INGRAM      The privy?

KIT      That's right.

INGRAM      Then by all means, continue.

KIT      Thank you for your blessing...What are you doing in my bushes?

BLOB      Admiring your lovely foliage.

*KIT shakes his head and leaves.*

INGRAM      Did you hear that? He's going to the privy.

BLOB      The Queen's Privy Council?

INGRAM      What else could he mean?

NICHOLAS        Why would he be going to the Queen's Privy Council?

INGRAM          It must have been that story we made up about Marlowe plotting treason.

NICHOLAS        Cripes! The Queen must be bringing him in for interrogation. We didn't factor this into the equation.

BLOB            You don't suppose he will rat on us, do you?

NICHOLAS        Of course he's going to rat on us! He is about to be interrogated by the Queen's Privy Council! They will torture him until he spills everything he knows!

BLOB            Marlowe knows everything we've done!

INGRAM          My embezzling.

BLOB            And the Babington Plot.

INGRAM          Bugger off, Blob.

NICHOLAS        They'll put Marlowe on the rack! Quarter him! Boil him! Disembowel him! He'll be sure to blurt something out!

INGRAM          Marlowe is a loose cannon. He must be silenced.

WILL            *(entering)* Kit! It's been longer than nine minutes! Where are you! *(notices spies)* Have you gentlemen in the bushes seen Kit? I don't understand what is taking him so long. I'm rather worried.

BLOB            Keep waiting. He won't be back any time soon.

NICHOLAS        He's being interrogated by the Queen's Privy Council.

WILL            No!

INGRAM          He's being charged for treason and will be tortured into confessing.

WILL            *(rushing back inside)* Fire and Brimstone!

NICHOLAS        What do you suppose we should do?

BLOB            Prepare to be hanged.

# Act One, Scene 10

*WILL is pacing around in KIT's apartment.*

*Enter KIT.*

WILL    Kit! Oh, Kit, thank God you're okay! You survived! Oh praise be to Heaven!

KIT     Will...

WILL    I want you to sit down and tell me all about it.

KIT     Why?

WILL    Come on, Kit. Give me details.

KIT     It's sort of personal.

WILL    Did it hurt?

KIT     What's that to the purpose?

WILL    It must have hurt. You did a dirty deed.

KIT     You're weird.

| | |
|---|---|
| WILL | How did it feel? |
| KIT | I don't know...Refreshing. |
| WILL | Refreshing? |
| KIT | As a matter of fact, it felt rather good to let it all out. |
| WILL | You let it ALL out? |
| KIT | That is the point. |
| WILL | I can't believe you did that. And with the Queen watching. |
| KIT | The Queen was watching? |
| WILL | Of course. She watches everything. |
| KIT | Even THAT? |
| WILL | You shouldn't have done it, Kit. You should have held it in. As painful as it might be. |
| KIT | It's not healthy to hold it in. |
| WILL | Tell me this...Did you let anything out that might have upset the Queen? |
| KIT | To be frank, I don't see how any of this is the Queen's business. A man's... *(gesturing towards his bowels)* internal affairs are private. |

| | |
|---|---|
| WILL | That's not what the Queen says. |
| KIT | I don't give a rat's ass what the Queen says! |
| WILL | *(shrieks)* I didn't hear you say that. |
| KIT | The Queen is a demented woman! |
| WILL | You are full of crap! |
| KIT | Not anymore, I'm not! |

*Enter THOMAS.*

| | |
|---|---|
| THOMAS | Kit, you forgot to empty the chamber pot again. |
| WILL | Chamber pot? |
| THOMAS | Must you forget to empty the chamber pot every time you go to the privy? |
| WILL | The priv...*(hides his face as he leaves)* Excuse me. |
| THOMAS | What's with him? |
| KIT | I don't know, but I learned a little more about the Queen than I needed to know. |
| THOMAS | Never mind. Just empty this chamber pot. I'm not doing it. |

*Exit KIT with chamber pot.*

THOMAS            *(to rat)* Can you believe that guy, Stiffy? He never empties the chamber pot. I'll bet he does that on purpose just to irk me. That is so like him.

*Knock at the door.*

OFFICER 1         Open up in the name of the Queen!

*THOMAS opens the door.*

THOMAS            What the...

OFFICER 2         Christopher Marlowe?

THOMAS            The name's Thomas Kyd.

OFFICER 2         Is this the residence of Christopher Marlowe?

THOMAS            He's my roommate.

OFFICER 1         Search the premises.

THOMAS            You can't come in here! This is private property!

OFFICER 1         We have a search warrant from the Queen.

*OFFICER 2 finds Atheist literature in the closet.*

OFFICER 2         I found something!

THOMAS            What?

OFFICER 2       Brochures of an Atheist nature. Along with some heretic accusations signed by one Richard Baines.

OFFICER 1       Do you know anything about this, Thomas Kyd?

THOMAS          I don't know anything!

OFFICER 2       He knows something. Take him away!

> *OFFICERS grab THOMAS and drag him out. THOMAS begs and screams "It was Kit!" repeatedly on the way out.*

*END OF ACT ONE*

# Act Two, Scene One

> *KIT enters the apartment. THOMAS is not there. He finds STIFFY lying in the middle of the floor.*

KIT          Stiffy? What are you doing here all alone? Thomas never goes anywhere without you...Something isn't right.

> *Door opens. WILL helps THOMAS walk in. THOMAS is in a full body bandage with only his eyes and mouth exposed. THOMAS walks in stiffly and with great difficulty.*

KIT          Thomas?

THOMAS      Kit, before you do anything to me, let me remind you that I am in a tremendous amount of pain.

KIT          I hate conversations that begin that way.

THOMAS      I would also like to say that I love you...in a purely platonic way.

KIT          What did you do?

THOMAS        Do? I, um…

WILL          He told the Queen you are an Atheist.

KIT           Thomas! Have you taken leave of your senses?

THOMAS        I didn't mean to, Kit! It just sort of slipped out while they were torturing me!

KIT           Do you know what they do to Atheists?

THOMAS        Um…the same thing they just did to me now?

KIT           Thomas!

THOMAS        They tortured me! Nearly to death!

KIT           Perhaps I should send you back so they can finish the job!

THOMAS        It's not as though they tickled it out of me! They put me on the rack! What did you expect me to say?

KIT           I don't know. The truth, maybe?

THOMAS        I tried the truth! I really did! But the truth wasn't interesting enough for them! They wouldn't stop torturing me until I told them what they wanted to hear!

KIT           What they wanted to hear?

THOMAS        They came here looking for you, Kit! For you! They searched the apartment and found those Atheist brochures we tossed in the closet. And some prank heretic notes that Dick wrote. You weren't around so they took me in to be interrogated. They asked me who the heretic literature belonged to, and I blurted out, "Marlowe! They belong to Christopher Marlowe!"

KIT               I know we've had our differences, but this...

THOMAS            They wouldn't stop until I gave them the right answer! They want you to be guilty! The Queen has it in her head that you are an Atheist, and once that woman has her mind set on something...

KIT               God save me!

THOMAS            They're coming to get you, Kit. *(knock at the door)* There they are.

OFFICER 1         *(from outside)* Open up in the name of the Queen!

KIT               Couldn't I open up in the name of someone else?

WILL              Just tell them what they want to hear. It will keep you out of trouble.

KIT               I suppose it has kept YOU out of trouble, hasn't it, Will?

OFFICER 2         Is Christopher Marlowe in there?

*KIT opens the door.*

KIT               I'm the man you want. How have I offended the Queen this time?

OFFICER 1    Treason.

OFFICER 2    Blasphemy.

KIT          Which one is it?

OFFICER 1    We'll let the Queen decide that.

OFFICER 2    Seize him!

>                    *The officers each seize KIT by each*
>                    *arm and begin to take him away.*

WILL         Wait! Don't take him away! *(straightens KIT's ruff and*
             *fixes his hair)*

KIT          Will, what are you doing?

WILL         You're seeing the Queen. You must look your best.

>                    *OFFICERS take KIT away.*

THOMAS       There goes a dead man.

WILL         It doesn't make any sense.

THOMAS       We are all players in the Queen's charade. The only
             thing we can do is recite our lines.

>                    *Enter CATHERINE and JOHN.*

CATHERINE          Kitty? Are you here?

JOHN               *(noticing THOMAS' bandages)* New outfit?

THOMAS             The rack.

JOHN               Ah.

CATHERINE          I brought Kitty some homemade mustard and cress juice in case he has scurvy.

JOHN               I told her she was being a mutton head.

CATHERINE          They say scurvy can cause irritability and make people loose control of their actions.

JOHN               If that's the case, Kit was born with scurvy.

CATHERINE          Has Kitty mentioned having any pains in his loins?

THOMAS             Um...Ms. Arthur?

CATHERINE          Have his teeth fallen out?

THOMAS             Kit isn't here.

CATHERINE          Where is he?

THOMAS             He's sort of being...tortured.

JOHN               What did he do this time?

THOMAS        He was charged with possession of heretic literature.

CATHERINE     (*throwing herself on the floor*) I've failed! I've failed!
              I've failed!

JOHN          (*shoving a shoe in her mouth*) Stuff it, Catherine.

# Act Two, Scene Two

*The stage is dark. KIT is spotlit, centre stage, facing the audience. He has an officer on either side of him. He is being questioned by the Queen. QUEEN is not visible. Only her voice is heard.*

KIT          So which is it? Treason or blasphemy?

QUEEN     They are the same.

KIT          What say you?

QUEEN     I am your Queen. If you reject God, you reject me.

KIT          I believe in God. But I don't believe in you. If that makes me an Atheist, then go ahead and torture me.

OFFICER 1  Treason!

OFFICER 2  Blasphemy!

QUEEN     I will ask you one more time. Are you an Atheist?

KIT          Not exactly.

QUEEN          Are you a Christian then?

KIT            I'm not sure.

QUEEN          Then what are you?

KIT            Confused!

QUEEN          What confuses you? You are either a Christian or you're not. Judging by your less than model lifestyle, all fingers seem to point at Atheism.

KIT            I know there's a God somewhere. I just don't know where to find him.

QUEEN          And you expect to find him in a tavern?

KIT            Why not? I can't find him anywhere else. Everywhere I turn I see blood and gore. Covert death plots. Loveless marriages. Espionage. For the love of Ud, people watch public hangings for fun!

QUEEN          The content in your plays is no better.

KIT            I'm only commenting on things that need to be changed.

OFFICER 1      Shall we hang him now, your majesty?

QUEEN          Let him finish.

KIT            Religion has nothing to do with God anymore. God has been replaced with a monarch. You have shoved God in a closet somewhere and taught us to forget about him.

QUEEN        I am God.

KIT        If that's the case, then you are the blasphemer. Not me.

QUEEN        You will be silenced. I shall have your ears cut off.

KIT        Why would you cut off my ears to silence me? I don't talk with my ears.

QUEEN        Did I give you permission to say such things?

KIT        You are not my puppet-master. I can say whatever I bloody well please without any prompting from Queen Elizabitch. Did I say that out loud?

QUEEN        Nobody has ever spoken to me in this manner. Unprecedented.

KIT        I don't do anything unless it's unprecedented.

OFFICER 1        Shall I call for the rack-master, your majesty?

KIT        Go ahead. I value the liberty of speech above my very life.

QUEEN        Enough of this privy-nip! You will report to court every day until your next date with the Privy Council. Don't leave town, Marlowe. I'm not done with you yet.

*OFFICERS take KIT away.*

# Act Two, Scene Three

*The apartment.*

THOMAS     I can't believe you called her Queen Elizabitch.

KIT        I can't explain it, Thomas. I open my mouth and these things just start flying out. It frightens me sometimes.

THOMAS     It might be scurvy.

KIT        Wha?

THOMAS     Your mother was here.

KIT        Oh.

WILL       How could you say such things to the Queen? What if it offended her?

KIT        That is the point, Will.

THOMAS     So that's what this was all about. You put on this big performance for the Queen just so you could get a rise out of her. This is so like you.

KIT        Thomas...

THOMAS      You wanted to see how mad you could get her before she tortured you. Do I know you or do I know you?

KIT         Thomas...

THOMAS      You always have to push boundaries, don't you, Kit? Challenge limitations. Well, if you're that dumb, you deserve to be tortured.

WILL        That wasn't very nice, Thomas.

KIT         I may have a big mouth, but every word that comes out of it is the truth.

                            *ANNE is heard screaming outside the door.*

ANNE        *(from outside)* Did I say you could touch me?

ROBERT      *(from outside)* You love it.

                            *Enter ANNE and ROBERT.*

THOMAS      Robert Greene? Wait. Didn't he die last year?

ANNE        Touch me again and I'll give you a bloody coxcomb!

ROBERT      I'm only taking what's mine.

WILL        Yours?

ROBERT      There's no point in letting a perfectly good set of knockers go to waste. After all, Shakespeare, you're not using them.

ANNE          Will, do something about this thug, will you?

WILL          I don't know if I can.

ANNE          And they said chivalry was dead.

KIT           Will, are you just going to stand there and let...

ROBERT        He won't do anything. He'd rather choke to death on the milk of human kindness than to stand up to me.

WILL          Mr. Greene?

ROBERT        He's afraid he would offend someone.

WILL          Mr. Greene?

ROBERT        And even if he had any testosterone, he's too much of a moron to figure out a good revenge plot.

WILL          Mr. Greene?

ROBERT        Yes. What?

WILL          Have you ever read *Arden of Feversham?*

ROBERT        The play written by the anonymous dramatist? I know it well.

WILL          Remember that really evil character in it named

Greene?

ROBERT    That greedy, selfish jackass who looks out for none but himself? What about him?

WILL    Who do you think wrote *Arden of Feversham?*

ROBERT    I just told you, it was anonym...You didn't.

WILL    Not bad for an illiterate bard.

ROBERT    You wrote a scandalous play and put me in it!

KIT    Way to go, Will!

ROBERT    First you steal my audience, now my reputation!

WILL    And you stole my wench! *(punches ROBERT in the face)*

> KIT, THOMAS and ANNE have identical looks of shock on their faces.

ROBERT    You hit me in the nose!

WILL    I would have gone for the balls, but you don't have any.

KIT    I knew you had it in you, Will!

ROBERT    *(noticing ANNE)* Ug! Get away from me, Strumpet!

ANNE    What the...

ROBERT        I will not touch something that William Shakespeare
              has touched! *(leaving)* You will never amount to
              anything, William Shakespeare! Never! *(exit)*

WILL          *(calling out to ROBERT)* I hope you won't take any of
              this personally, Mr. Greene!

ANNE          You rescued me, my adorable, little Willie Woo Woo!

KIT           Willie Woo Woo?

WILL          She calls me that sometimes.

ANNE          Come here, you! *(grabs WILL by the sides of his head
              and kisses him aggressively on the mouth)*

                        *WILL looks stunned for a moment
                        and then passes out.*

ANNE          Not this again.

                        *ANNE flings WILL over her
                        shoulder and carries him out.*

KIT           Now THAT'S drama.

THOMAS        Kit! You have darker matters to concern yourself with.

KIT           I don't want to think about it. I may only have a couple
              of weeks left and I want to savour them.

THOMAS        Have you thought about skipping town? Assuming a
              new identity?

KIT          I thought about it. But it's a stupid idea. I am a high profile man. Someone would eventually discover me.

THOMAS    So what are you going to do?

KIT          Stop ambushing me, will you? I just want to get my mind off things. In fact, I've made plans to have dinner with some friends in Debtford Friday next.

THOMAS    You have friends?

KIT          Ingram Frizer, Nicholas Skeres and Blob Poley.

THOMAS    You're not supposed to leave town. Furthermore, do you think it's safe to be seen in public?

KIT          I will be safe as long as I'm in the company of friends.

# Act Two, Scene Four

> *The tavern of MADAM ELEANOR BULL. KIT, INGRAM, NICHOLAS and BLOB are seated around a table.*

NICHOLAS      Perk up, Kit.

BLOB      Yeah. You look like death.

> *BLOB gets kicked from under the table.*

INGRAM      The whole point of this evening is to help you get your mind off things. How about a game of backgammon?

MADAM BULL      Wine, Gentlemen!

BLOB      Wine? We want ale, Eleanor!

MADAM BULL      Wine is better for toasting. And you may call me Madam Bull.

NICHOLAS & BLOB      Ooooo. Madam.

BLOB      Not just a wench, but a classy wench.

NICHOLAS    She is practically royalty.

MADAM BULL    Not quite royalty. Let's just say I have court connections.

INGRAM    *(pulling MADAM BULL on his lap)* Come here, Madam Bull.

MADAM BULL    A toast! To cousin Blanche. God rest her soul. *(bursts into laughter followed by the others who do the same)*

KIT    Who's cousin Blanche?

MADAM BULL    She was the Queen's chief gentlewoman and confidante. Good old Blanche finally kicked off and left me in her will.

INGRAM    Ching, ching.

MADAM BULL    That's not all she left me. She also left me in the Queen's favour.

NICHOLAS    To the Queen!

    *They all raise their glasses in a toast, except KIT.*

INGRAM    Kit?

KIT    *(no enthusiasm, still not raising his glass)* Klink.

INGRAM    There's just no pleasing you, is there, Kit? Here we invite you to Debtford for a nice evening of gluttony and drunkenness and all you do is mope. And Madam Bull was so kind as to offer us a room for the enire day for a sum of pence.

MADAM BULL    What do you mean kind? I'm the one who gets to be surrounded by four devastatingly handsome men. *(to BLOB)* Except maybe you.

KIT    Are we here to eat or not?

MADAM BULL    Then there's this one. *(drapes her arms around KIT from behind and talks into his ear)*

KIT    Me?

MADAM BULL    You're my favourite.

> *INGRAM, NICHOLAS and BLOB pound on the table and make animal noises.*

KIT    Madam, please.

MADAM BULL    Where did you get such pretty clothes?

KIT    I'm hungry.

MADAM BULL    So am I.

> *INGRAM, NICHOLAS and BLOB howl like dogs. KIT peels MADAM BULL off of himself.*

KIT            Terrific. Starve me to death. I'll be spared of the Privy Council.

INGRAM         He gets irritable when he's deprived of food.

BLOB           Me too. Food, Wench!

NICHOLAS       *(grabbing MADAM BULL's hindquarters)* She's not a wench. She's a madam.

MADAM BULL     Alright already. I'm taking orders.

BLOB           It's Wednesday. Fish night!

INGRAM         I'll have an order of eel.

NICHOLAS       I'll have the cockle and lamprey combo.

MADAM BULL     Do you want filberts or field mushrooms with that?

BLOB           How are your oysters?

MADAM BULL     They smell a bit off tonight.

BLOB           I'll take two dozen.

KIT            Pork please.

               *Everyone stops and gives KIT a look of shock.*

BLOB           But, Kit. It's fish night.

KIT          I want pork.

NICHOLAS      But everyone orders fish on Wednesdays.

KIT          Right. And I'm ordering pork.

INGRAM      Always has to be different.

*Exit MADAM BULL.*

KIT          I have to pee. *(gets up)* Before I go, I just wanted to thank you guys for doing this for me. I've been an ogre all day, taking things out on you. I don't say this often, so savour it. Sometimes I feel like you guys are my only friends. The only constant thing in my twisted life. There aren't many people who I trust but... Hell. I really have to pee. *(leaves)*

NICHOLAS      Anyone feel guilty right about now?

*After a brief pause, they all burst into laughter.*

INGRAM      Betraying a good friend makes us all the more skilled as spies.

BLOB        Remember the Creed of Spies?

*They put their hands on their hearts and recite in unison.*

ALL          A spy is dedicated to the eternal promise to protect, uphold and defend the life and dignities of her majesty the Queen, and to take pride in the loyalties thereof. To live for the Queen. To die for the Queen. Until someone else gives us a better offer.

INGRAM          We must follow through with our plan. Marlowe must be killed. Otherwise, he'll surely reveal unflattering information about us when he is being tortured.

BLOB            Who will do the deed?

NICHOLAS        Blob and I are the most experienced in death plots.

INGRAM          Fie! What makes you think I can't do it!

NICHOLAS        Ingram, we never said...

INGRAM          You don't think I have it in me! You don't think I'm a good enough spy to betray my own friend!

NICHOLAS        Ingram, haven't I always said that when it comes to money-lending, you are the devil incarnate?

BLOB            You don't have to prove anything to us, so get this chip off your shoulder.

INGRAM          I'll prove to you how worthy I am to bear the Creed of Spies. I will do the deed!

NICHOLAS        Whatever...

INGRAM          I have the entire conspiracy worked out in my head. We will distract Marlowe by starting a heated argument.

BLOB            No challenge there. It's easy to get Marlowe angry.

INGRAM          Who here is in charge of the plot, you or m…

                          *INGRAM notices MADAM BULL nervously skulking about. She is conspicuously carrying a dagger.*

INGRAM          Madam Bull?

MADAM BULL      Dagger? What dagger?

BLOB            What would a madam need with a dagger?

MADAM BULL      Okay, you caught me. I was going to use this dagger to kill Christopher Marlowe.

NICHOLAS        Whatever for?

MADAM BULL      As a favour to the Queen. She wants him dead because he humiliated her when he was being questioned.

NICHOLAS        Why doesn't she wait a few days and have the Privy Council order his murder?

MADAM BULL      It would make her look bad. After all, Marlowe was once in the Queen's secret service. She'd like to have people think that she treats her employees well. Besides, who knows what scandalous things Marlowe would say about the Queen while under torture? Marlowe's mouth has a mind of its own.

INGRAM          That's for sure.

MADAM BULL    Who's to say Marlowe wouldn't curse and defy the Queen right there in front of everyone? Independent thinkers are dangerous. Others might follow Marlowe's lead and before you know it, there could be a series of treasonous plots against Elizabeth's life. Marlowe must be silenced before the trial.

NICHOLAS    This is such a co-incidence. We were just about to murder Marlowe too!

INGRAM    Me. I was the one who was...

BLOB    This saves us a lot of trouble. Madam Bull can do the dirty work and we won't run the risk being hanged.

INGRAM    You all hate me! You think I'm a mockery to spies everywhere! What reason have I to live!

NICHOLAS    On second thought, maybe you should let Ingram do the deed, Madam Bull. He has some self-esteem issues. It might help him in the healing process.

MADAM BULL    By all means. I'm a sucker for vulnerable men. Would you like to use my dagger, Ingram?

INGRAM    I have my own dagger right here in my stocking.

BLOB    Shhh! Kit's coming!

*Enter KIT.*

INGRAM    Oh! Am I stuffed!

KIT            But our food hasn't arrived yet.

BLOB         You took too long. We ate already. Yours too.

MADAM BULL    *(caressing KIT's face)* You are such a handsome one. Those brown eyes. It's such a waste. *(kisses him)*

KIT            What means this lady?

NICHOLAS     Someone has to take care of this bill.

KIT            This one's on me, gentlemen.

BLOB         What do you mean, on you? We ate your meal.

KIT            It's the least I can do after the way I've snapped at you.

NICHOLAS     But I wanted to pay for dinner tonight!

KIT            Put your purse away, Nicholas.

NICHOLAS     MAKE ME!

                         *INGRAM creeps up behind KIT.*

KIT            I'm trying to be nice here!

BLOB         There will be no niceness in this tavern! I am paying the bill!

                         *INGRAM pulls dagger from his stocking.*

NICHOLAS        Take one more coin out, and you'll be swallowing it!

KIT             You paid last time, you bastard!

NICHOLAS        Say that to my face!

                              *INGRAM assumes the position to plunge the dagger into KIT.*

BLOB            Give me that bill, you ruffian!

KIT             Your money is no good here!

                              *Lights go out. Arguing continues.*

BLOB            You want to take this outside!

KIT             Maybe I do!

NICHOLAS        Why I oughta'...

MADAM BULL      Kit! Look out behind you!

                              *MADAM BULL lets out a blood curdling scream.*

# Act Two, Scene Five

*The apartment. THOMAS is still in his full body bandage. WILL is pacing.*

WILL        It's been three days since Kit went to Debtford. Where in the world is he?

THOMAS      It was rather rude of you not to see your wife off when she left for Stratford. You may never see her that amorous again.

WILL        I'm worried here. It's been three days.

*Enter DICK.*

DICK        Have you heard?

THOMAS      We don't have the patience for you right now, Dick.

DICK        If you give me five ducats, I'll tell you what I know.

THOMAS      That'll take all of three seconds.

DICK        Christopher Marlowe is dead.

*THOMAS and WILL stop and look*

*shocked. After a short pause,*
*WILL begins weeping hysterically.*

THOMAS        What happened?

DICK          Five ducats.

THOMAS        I'll give you five kicks in the head if you don't tell me.

DICK          He was stabbed in a tavern brawl. I don't know all the details, but I hear that it was all Kit's fault.

THOMAS        It always is. You know nothing more?

DICK          Only that the murderer claims he did it in self-defense.

## Act Two, Scene Six

*The stage is black. In the centre of the stage is a spotlight which illuminates DANBY the coroner, OFFICER 1 and the body of KIT on a slab. There is a sheet over the body with a dagger sticking out of the place where the head would be.*

DANBY          Self-defense?

OFFICER 1      That's what the Queen says.

DANBY          But I've read the witness' report and...

OFFICER 1      The Queen says it was self-defense. Don't make her a liar.

DANBY          I am a coroner. Not a miracle worker.

OFFICER 1      Danby, you are the Queen's coroner. Do what the Queen says.

DANBY          Why wasn't the local coroner in Debtford notified? The Queen's coroner isn't supposed to be involved unless the murder took place within twelve miles of the

Queen's person. The Queen was at Nonsuch Palace in Surrey the night of the murder.

OFFICER 1      Stop asking questions. Just have something intelligent for the trial. We need a coroner's inquest.

*Exit OFFICER 1.*

DANBY      I am a dead man. This witness' report is full of inconsistencies. There's no way this could have been self-defense. Come on, Danby. Think of something.

*Lights change colour and DANBY is at the trial.*

DANBY      Gentlemen. I have prepared the coroner's report. The murder weapon cost twelve pence.

OFFICER 1      The body, Danby.

DANBY      Yes. The body is dead.

OFFICER 1      Danby, your testimony?

DANBY      *(deep breath)* The dagger, belonging to one Ingram Frizer, entered the victim's brain through the entry of the right eye. I know what you're thinking. How could this be done in self-defense if the victim was stabbed in the face with the murderer's own weapon, which had been moments earlier, sheathed in Frizer's stocking? There is a logical explanation. I have choreographed the entire episode in my head and have come up with what I call *The Magic Dagger Theory*. Since the deed was done in self-defense, we know that Marlowe drew arms first. After a dispute over the dinner bill, Marlowe and Frizer got into a struggle. The magic dagger unsheathed itself from Frizer's stocking, floated through the air and landed in Marlowe's hand. Marlowe, being the AGGRESSOR with the INTENT to kill, used the BLUNT end of the dagger to thwack Frizer on the back of the head. It was not difficult for Marlowe to reach the back of Frizer's head while being pinned down to a bar table, because Marlowe has abnormally long arms and convenient, rubbery elbows.

OFFICER 1    Danby, your story is entirely speculative...I like it. Next witness. Madam Eleanor Bull.

MADAM BULL    He did it! He's the one! Ingram Frizer murdered Christopher Marlowe in cold blood!

OFFICER 1    We'll pretend we didn't hear that. Next witnesses. Ingram Frizer, Nicholas Skeres and Robert Poley.

MADAM BULL    Wait a minute. Ingram Frizer can't be a defendant AND a witness.

OFFICER 1    What do you mean? Our law has no guidelines for evidence. If we do things right, this murder trial won't take more than ten minutes.

> *MADAM BULL exits indignantly. INGRAM, NICHOLAS and BLOB each sit on a stool, facing the audience.*

OFFICER 1    Where was Christopher Marlowe stabbed?

INGRAM          In the eye.

NICHOLAS        In the brain.

BLOB            In the tavern.

OFFICER 1       *(after giving BLOB  an odd look)* Where did the murder take place?

INGRAM          A tavern.

NICHOLAS        A brothel.

BLOB            The home of Eleanor Bull.

OFFICER 1       What was the motive?

INGRAM          The dinner bill.

NICHOLAS        A gambling debt.

BLOB            Suicide.

OFFICER 1       Who's idea was it to kill Marlowe?

INGRAM          The spymaster.

NICHOLAS        A rival in love.

BLOB            Some guy named Frances.

OFFICER 1       Thank you, gentlemen. That clears everything up nicely. The final testimony will be from Christopher Marlowe. *(to corpse)* Mr. Marlowe, do you have anything to say in your defense? *(puts ear to corpse)* He has nothing to say in his defense...Now then, what says her majesty?

QUEEN          I am granting Frances Freezer a pardon on the grounds of self-defense.

OFFICER 1      Who's Frances Freezer?

INGRAM         Yes! I got away with it! I am a very good spy!

>                    *INGRAM stops to find he is getting odd looks from everyone around him.*

## Act Two, Scene Seven

*The apartment. WILL is alone.*

WILL            Something isn't right...Something...

*Enter MADAM BULL.*

MADAM BULL    Hello?

WILL            Who are you?

MADAM BULL    Eleanor Bull. Who are you?

WILL            William Shakespeare.

MADAM BULL    William Shakepeare? Kit spoke very highly of you.

WILL            He...he did?

MADAM BULL    I brought Kit's hat. I thought someone might want it. I found it in my rooming house the night he was...

WILL            It was your rooming house? You saw what happened?

MADAM BULL    I have to go now.

WILL          You know something, don't you?

MADAM BULL   I saw nothing!

WILL          He was my friend!

MADAM BULL   I'm sorry this happened! I didn't know how fond I'd become of...

WILL          Was it self-defense? Did Kit try to...

MADAM BULL   It was the blunt end of the dagger!...When Kit hit Ingram on the head. He used the blunt end of the dagger. You figure it out.

*Exit MADAM BULL.*

WILL          The blunt end of the dagger. If Kit wanted to kill Ingram, he would have used the blade. Ingram wasn't trying to defend himself. Kit was.

*KIT's ghost appears.*

KIT          Did I hear my name?

WILL          Kit! What are you doing here?

KIT          Is that any way to talk to a dead friend?

WILL          Don't you know it's a felony to conjure spirits? I could get in deep trouble if someone finds you here!

KIT    You did not conjure me. I came on my own.

WILL    Why?

KIT    Will, you are a nice guy. So nice, in fact, that it is quite irritating. Niceness offends people in this backwards world. But people like to be offended. It gives them something to complain about.

WILL    What are you trying to say?

KIT    I wanted to change the world, Will. You do it for me.

WILL    I have so many things to thank you for.

KIT    Whatever it is, your welcome. I have to go.

WILL    Where are you going?

KIT    *(mischievous grin)* Heaven.

WILL    Heaven?  But I thought...

KIT    You know how I love to shock people.

WILL    How wondrous!

KIT    One more thing. Look after my mom. She doesn't take things like this very well.

WILL    Go figure.

> *KIT disappears. THOMAS enters with great difficulty, still in his full body bandage.*

THOMAS          Did I hear voices in here?

WILL            Thomas! You'll never guess what I just saw! I...

THOMAS          What? You saw what?

WILL            A spider. I saw a spider run across the floor.

THOMAS          Try not to get too excited, Will. You wouldn't want to overexert yourself.

> *CATHERINE and JOHN can be heard outside the door. CATHERINE is wailing and weeping.*

JOHN            *(from outside)* For the love of Ud, Catherine! Would you stop being so dramatic? You're creating a spectacle!

> *Enter CATHERINE and JOHN. CATHERINE throws herself on the floor.*

CATHERINE       My baby boy! My baby boy! My baby boy!

JOHN            Smeck up, Catherine! You must have seen this coming!

THOMAS          Marlowe himself couldn't have written a more tragic ending.

CATHERINE     Oh, grief! Oh, misery!

JOHN          *(moaning)* Oh, Catherine. Would you believe she was outside, digging her own grave this morning?

CATHERINE     My adorable baby boy, with his big, brown eyes and squeezable cheeks!

WILL          Ms. Arthur? If I tell you something, do you promise never to tell a soul?

CATHERINE     Starting tomorrow I'm taking an oath of silence.

JOHN          I'll believe that when I see it.

WILL          Kit is not dead.

CATHERINE     What?

WILL          He faked his death and is hiding in a secret place.

CATHERINE     You mean to say...

WILL          He's writing my plays for me now.

CATHERINE     Kitty is not dead?

WILL          You have to be sure never to blow his cover. He's hiding from the Queen.

JOHN            See, Catherine? Didn't I say you were overreacting?

CATHERINE       Oh! Thanks be to Heaven!

WILL            Not so loud! It's a secret!

                                *Exit CATHERINE and JOHN.*

THOMAS          Now you've done it.

WILL            Kit wouldn't have wanted his mother to grieve. It was one, little fib for the greater good. Besides, I made Catherine promise not to tell anyone.

THOMAS          Will, if you want news to spread fast, just tell Catherine Arthur.

CATHERINE       *(from outside)* MY BABY BOY IS ALIVE!

                                *A look of terror comes over WILL's face*

                                *FINIS*